SURVIVOR DIARIES

LOST!

SURVIVOR DIARIES

LOST!

By Terry Lynn Johnson

HOUGHTON MIFFLIN HARCOURT
Boston   New York

hmhco.com

The text was set in Adobe Caslon Pro.
Illustrations by Jani Orban

Library of Congress Cataloging-in-Publication Data
Names: Johnson, Terry Lynn, author. | Orban, Jani, illustrator.
Title: Lost! / by Terry Lynn Johnson ; illustrated by Jani Orban.
Description: Boston ; New York : Houghton Mifflin Harcourt, [2018] | Series:
Survivor diaries | Summary: In an interview with a reporter,
eleven-year-old Carter recounts his tale of survival with twelve-year-old
Anna in the perilous jungles of Costa Rica. Includes a list of suvival kit items.
Identifiers: LCCN 2017010165 | ISBN 9780544971189 paper over board |
ISBN 9781328519078 paperback
Subjects: | CYAC: Survival—Fiction. | Jungles—Fiction. | Costa Rica—Fiction.
Classification: LCC PZ7.J63835 Lo 2018 | DDC [Fic]—dc23
LC record available at https://lccn.loc.gov/2017010165

Printed in the United States of America
DOC 10 9 8 7 6 5 4 3 2
4500722950

For Christal, who got me out of that tree.

CHAPTER ONE

"Tell me, Carter. How did you survive being lost in the rainforest?" the reporter asked. He pressed Record on his phone.

I spun on my barstool and raised my arms out like a California condor. Or maybe a trumpeter swan would be more appropriate. They have the largest body mass of any North American bird.

"Did you talk with Anna?" I asked.

"I'll be meeting with her tomorrow." The reporter rolled up his sleeves and then produced a notepad and pen from his shirt pocket. "I want your version of what happened in Costa

Rica," he continued. "This interview is for the Survivor Diaries I'm writing. About kids like you making it out of life-threatening situations. You're younger than Anna, only eleven years old, right?"

"Yeah—" I jumped at the squeal behind me, but it was just one of the little kids that Mom babysits.

Mom scooped her up. "Time for a nap, I think. I'll be right back." She headed for the stairs. I hoped she noticed I had only jumped a tiny bit.

Thinking back to my time in the jungle, I dried my palms across my red sweatpants. Red like the breast feathers of the resplendent quetzal. The bird that started it all. Adding that endangered bird to my life list—all the different bird species I've seen—nearly *ended* my life.

"All right." The reporter rubbed his hairless head and then looked at me expectantly. "Tell me what happened."

"The monkeys," I began. "Their calls were so

terrifying. Howler monkeys make such an eerie noise because of a bone they have in their throat. You can hear them three miles away. Did you know they're the loudest of all the New World monkeys? That's what freaked out Anna. They were leaping overhead. The branches of the trees shook all around us. We could hear the roaring, coming closer—"

"What monkeys?" The reporter's long forehead wrinkled in confusion. "Carter, start at the beginning."

I sighed. "It all started with licking an ancient statue."

CHAPTER TWO

Six weeks earlier. Osa Peninsula, Costa Rica.

Dad had suggested I hang out with Anna. Her family was also staying at Cabinas el Corcovado for March break. He thought it would be good for me to hang around someone my own age. Except Anna was in *seventh* grade, and I was as tall as her armpit, even wearing hiking boots. She'd never talk to someone like me if we were at school.

"Hey, this looks interesting." Anna pointed

to a trail marked by a fading sign with the word CASCADA. It had a photo of a waterfall with a carved stone statue of a monster next to it. "What is this thing?"

"*La Mona*." I read the words on the fence with a big arrow.

"Oh, I know that one!" she said. "That's the monkey-witch legend. She roams the forests in search of her missing kids and kills victims with bloodcurdling screams from the treetops."

Anna's family had been there a few days before we arrived, so she felt the need to educate me with all sorts of local legends she'd heard. They weren't even birders; they just came to relax.

My parents and I were there to see the resplendent quetzal. The Osa Peninsula had four hundred species of birds. Since we'd arrived in Costa Rica, we'd added the summer tanager, social flycatcher, bare-throated tiger-heron, and cinnamon hummingbird to our life lists. And there at the resort we'd seen a chestnut-mandibled toucan, and lots of scarlet macaws. Still no quetzals.

"The parental units are still busy with happy hour," Anna said. "We've got time before dinner. You want to do some exploring? Let's go see the waterfall! Legend has it, if you lick the statue there, you're blessed with strength. Don't you need some of that, Carter?"

"Lick the statue?" I asked. "Do you think you should be licking anything? They've got poison dart frogs here. They're one of the Earth's most toxic species. They have enough poison to kill twenty thousand mice!"

She stared at me.

"What?" I said, defensively.

"So weird," Anna muttered as she started down the trail. "Hey!" She ducked behind the fence post and came up brandishing a machete with a black handle. "Look what I found!" She gave it a few practice swings. "This thing is deadly. Someone must've left it here for protection against La Mona. Come on! Let's go before it gets too dark to find the statue."

I knew the part about licking the statue wasn't true. I'd never heard of that, not in any of the guidebooks I read before our trip. Anna had to be making it up.

But what if she wasn't? What if it did give you strength?

I clutched the binoculars around my neck and glanced toward the resort. A burst of laughter came from the pool. My parents never worried about me. I worried enough for everyone.

"Carter, you coming?"

I peered into the branches and imagined all the horrible things that could go wrong by following a marked trail into the jungle. I was shaking my head to refuse, when I saw it. I froze.

"What?" Anna asked, looking in the direction I was facing. But she didn't see the male resplendent quetzal until I raised a shaking hand and pointed.

"Three hundred and eight," I whispered.

"Huh?"

"That's how many different bird species I have on my life list," I said.

The quetzal was perched not far off the trail. Through my binoculars, he was even more brilliant than in pictures. His bright red belly was set off by the intense green glitter of his head and neck. I could pick out the sheen of blue and violet in his long tail.

"The quetzal was the spiritual protector of Mayan chiefs, helping them in battle," I said, eager to share the only legend I knew. "They say the quetzal sat on the chest of the dying warrior Uman and dipped its feathers in his blood. That's how it got the red." I wiped at the sweat running into my eyes. "Now it's endangered because of losing its habitat."

Anna didn't seem impressed. "Monkey statue that makes you strong is way more interesting."

"How could that be more interesting than finding an endangered bird?" And I didn't know why she was so interested in strength. I'd watched her pick up her dad in a piggyback race we had last night. She was taller and stronger than any girl I'd ever met.

The quetzal jumped off the branch and flew down the trail. I followed after it. Anna hacked at every plant unfortunate enough to be within striking distance of her machete.

"Watch where you swing that," I couldn't help saying. "The first rule of the rainforest is never touch before you can see. There are all sorts of dangerous things hiding in the leaves, like bushmasters."

"What's a bushmaster?" Anna asked. "They sound awesome."

"Bushmasters are venomous snakes. But the bigger threat is the fer-de-lance. They're extremely aggressive. Half of all snake bites are from the fer-de-lance, and they could be hiding anywhere."

When I noticed how far we'd come down the trail, I felt the familiar sensation of my heart racing, of my pulse speeding. I tried to control my breathing and think of something else. I did not have time for a panic attack.

Anna pretended to cough, and I heard the words, "Nerd alert." Then she began to flail her arms around, swatting at something near her head. She whipped a can of insect repellent from her pocket and sprayed the air furiously.

"I hate bugs," she said. "Why do you know all this stuff, anyway?"

"I read about it before we got here," I said. What I didn't explain was why. I didn't want to tell her how I had what my doctor called *anxiety*. And how I'd found the only way to control my attacks was to read as much as I could and be prepared, so I didn't worry about all the disasters waiting to happen.

The sound of running water got our attention. "The falls!" Anna announced.

The falls weren't that remarkable, more like a feeble cascade spilling over a log and pooling in a stream next to the trail. And beside the trail was a statue of a crouching stone monkey.

It wasn't as big as it had appeared in the photo. It was just a lump of greenish carved rock with moss or something growing on its head. It did not look like anyone should lick it.

Anna raced up to it first. I thought for sure she was just going to make me do it and then laugh at how dumb I was.

"Don't," I said, as she stuck her tongue out and dragged it across the statue.

She flexed her arms. "Your turn." She made a face, spat something out, and then patted the stone head. "Gritty."

My guts tightened. Now I *had* to do it.

I bent my head. The green parts did *not* look safe. Anna watched as I rubbed a spot clean on its shoulder, and then quickly touched it with my tongue. I wiped my tongue off with my finger and then raised my arms in triumph, proud of myself. Sadly, I did not feel any stronger.

That was when I realized how dark it was getting. With the canopy of the forest, not much sun trickled through. The trees had vines and strange things hanging off them that looked creepier and thicker the darker it got.

Anna seemed to notice at the same time. "We should head back," she said.

But just as we turned, we heard a terrifying noise. It sounded like a lion's roar or a grizzly bear about to charge.

CHAPTER THREE

The trees and branches above us came to life. With all that noise, I expected to see something huge emerge. But it was all coming from small animals with black furry bodies. They howled at us while leaping from branch to branch, shaking the leaves.

Anna let out a scream and then dove off the trail. She started lurching forward through the brush of the jungle.

"No!" I ran after her, my heart crashing in terror at this disaster. "It's just—"

Anna screamed as a seed ball hit her in the

back. More things rained down, making us cover our heads as we ran. I didn't know what was being thrown at us.

"She's coming for us," Anna was shrieking. "La Mona!"

I had to stop her!

Branches smacked me in the face. We darted this way and that, zigzagging through the openings between the trees. The monkeys chased us the whole time, shrieking, howling, shaking branches. It was like being in a Jurassic Park movie.

A leafy twig hurtled from above and landed on Anna's head. She went nuts, screeching and stamping her feet. The branch ripped away, and she sprinted again.

"Stop! Wait!"

Finally, she slowed down. We stood together panting, our chests heaving. Anna was soaked in sweat. Her blond hair was dark at the ends and stuck to her face.

"Never run in the jungle!" I yelled.

"What was that?" Anna asked.

"I tried to tell you," I gasped, catching my breath in the muggy heat. "They were just howler monkeys. We don't have to be afraid of monkeys."

We jumped at the horrifying noise right above us. Dark shapes shook the branches. Their howls reverberated through my bones. They filled the whole world with their deafening calls.

My skin prickled as they finally moved away and left us alone.

Anna peered up at the canopy. "I thought it was La Mona from that stupid story at first. But then I thought it was jaguars."

"We don't have to be afraid of jaguars either. The creatures to fear in the rainforest are venomous snakes and spiders. The way to avoid them is never run through the jungle."

Now that the risk of immediate death was over, the tension in me started to drain. I looked around at the unfriendly jungle and realized we were far from the trail. "Uh, do you know which way we came?"

Anna pointed, and I followed her for a while, weaving in and out of skinny trees, brushing aside dangling vines. I stepped into a spiderweb —its sticky threads clinging to my face nearly sent me into a full-blown panic attack.

Not a funnel-web spider. Not going to die horribly. I'm good. I let out a deep breath.

We walked past tall roots that grew like snaking eels, anchoring one giant tree from all sides. Smaller roots twisted across the ground in front of us.

"Don't step over roots, step on them," I reminded her. "So you don't surprise a snake."

Anna gave a root a whack with her machete. Suddenly she stopped, looked around, and headed in a different direction.

The worry churning my guts intensified. "Anna, stop. Listen to me. Do you know where we are? Do you know where the trail is?"

She definitely seemed nervous now. "I thought it was right here."

"You mean we're lost?" I said.

The distant calls of howler monkeys shook the jungle.

CHAPTER FOUR

"We have to stop," I said, panic rising. "If you get lost, you should stay where you are — *S. T. O. P.* means you should *stop, think, observe,* and *plan.* They'll be looking for us at the resort." I didn't know if I was reassuring Anna or myself. "If we stay here, they can probably track us."

"No way," Anna argued. "We're in the middle of the jungle. They'll never find us here. We have to keep going while we still have enough light to see." She pulled the loose hair off the back of her neck. "I'm older than you. I make the decisions. And I'm thirsty. We should see if we can find those falls again."

"Anna, listen to me," I said.

"I just want to be back at the resort." Anna wiped her forehead unhappily. She cupped a hand around her mouth and yelled, "Hey! Anyone? Can anyone hear us? We're in here!"

"Hellooooooo!" I yelled.

We listened a moment, but heard no response.

The heat and humidity in the air was like a pulsing, living thing. You could almost touch it. And we were soaked with sweat from all of the running. I was thankful my long-sleeved shirt kept the sharp branches from scraping me, but it clung to my arms. My pants stuck to my legs.

"The waterfall was around here somewhere. We should be able to find that stream," Anna said.

Her face was red and shiny. She continued walking, and I followed, but it was getting harder to see ahead. Our situation was spiraling out of my control. My hands started to shake.

"We can't keep going," I said again, slapping at a mosquito tickling my neck. "We should stop and make a fire so they can find us."

I took out the kit I always carried in my pocket in a Ziploc. Just holding it settled me. Anna watched. "What is that?"

"I made this for emergencies," I explained.

This one little thing was the reason I was able to go anywhere. Before I'd made the kit, I could barely leave the house. I kept imagining getting lost, being mugged, kidnapped. But my number one fear was being caught in a hurricane. As soon as I grew up, I was moving from Fort Meyers. Why would anyone want to live where spiraling winds up to two hundred miles an hour could bring a storm surge that would wipe out your neighborhood?

"With this kit," I said, "I've planned for every possible emergency. Fire starter, aluminum foil square, ground tarp, multitool, sewing kit, duct tape, signal mirror, micro flashlight, bandages, antiseptic towelette, emergency whistle, water purification tablet."

"All that is crammed in there?" Anna asked.

"Yup. And I'm wearing my paracord bracelet." I pointed at the dark green bracelet I'd made myself. "We're going to be okay."

I scanned the area around us as I popped open the Ziploc to find the flashlight. "We can try to clear the brush and make a fire here. Start building a shelter. We just have to find a water source to—"

A racket from the trees above interrupted my thoughts. Howlers again? I peered through the leaves to see a flash of white scampering down the trunk of a large tree next to us.

"Oh! It's white-faced monkeys!" Anna said. "We saw more of these at breakfast. They stole our bananas."

A few monkeys inched close to us on the

ground. While I was looking at one of them, another one abruptly lunged and snatched my kit right from my hands. I stared for a shocked moment, watching the monkey bound away. Then my brain finally caught up. "No! He's got my kit!"

The monkey scampered back up the tree, screeching the whole time, clutching my kit in one hand. He sat on a branch high above my head and inspected his prize.

"Give that back!" My voice cracked with desperation.

The monkey peeked in the bag and pulled out the lighter. He rolled it in his hands taking thoughtful little bites. Another monkey stole the kit from the monkey with the lighter. Holding it in his mouth, he raced away. Their screeching snapped my nerves.

"Stop it!"

But something had dropped from the tree. I bolted forward and picked up the small square

of plastic. I held it in my shaking fingers. The only thing I had left of my emergency kit was this folded up garbage bag. All of my careful preparations gone.

My heart pounded.

My breathing sped up. I choked down a sob. Sweat dripped off me. My body trembled. I felt walled in by the dense, dark jungle.

Please no. *Do not panic.*

"What's wrong with you?" Anna asked. "Are you okay? Here, you should sit down." She took my arm and led me to a hollow log. I stumbled after her. Anna was right. I needed to just breathe.

I reached into the leaves to clear a space to sit down, not thinking. And snatched my hand back with a yelp. We both saw something scuttle away.

A scorpion the size of a bow tie, with its stinger curled over its back.

"I'm gonna die!" I hollered.

Focus. Breathe in—one, hold, breathe out—two. Not working. Throat closing.

Smothering.

Black.

CHAPTER FIVE

When I came to, Anna was kneeling next to me.

"You're awake," she said in relief. Then she peered into my face. "Carter. Are you okay?" She pronounced each word slowly and loudly, as if I was an alien visiting the planet.

I nodded.

"You just started shaking like you were having a seizure or something, and I thought you died."

"I get panic attacks." I raised my hand to see where I'd been stung. As soon as I moved, I noticed the pain. It was like nothing I'd ever felt.

My whole body felt hot, but especially my hand where the scorpion had stung me.

"So you passing out like that wasn't from the scorpion?" Anna asked.

"Not sure ... This happens sometimes." I sounded funny. "But my lips are tingly."

"That's not good, is it?" Anna asked. "Are scorpions venomous like the bushmaster?"

"S-some are more dangerous than others." I had to calm down. Had to think. What did I know about scorpion stings? Some were fatal. I had no first aid kit. My brain was still jumbled from my panic attack, and I felt like I was about to have another one.

It began to rain.

"Your face is getting red." Anna hovered, worried. "I'm sorry, Carter!" she blurted out. "I didn't know that scorpion was there. I'm sorry I made you get stung!"

I couldn't form the words to respond.

Anna glanced around and then pointed to the palms beside us. "You were talking about making a shelter. Could we make a shelter with those big leaves?"

I nodded, or at least I think I did. I felt like I had a bobblehead, like my skull wasn't really attached to my body.

Anna hacked the giant fronds, which were as tall as her.

I tried to lace my fingers together like lattice. "Like this," I mumbled. I wished I wasn't lying in wet leaves. Were any more scorpions hiding in the dark? What else was crawling around us?

The pain was overwhelming. I squeezed my eyes shut and hugged my hand that had been stung.

Mosquitos attacked next. They flitted across our faces, into our eyes, up our noses. They buzzed in my ears. Drove me mad. Mosquitos carry all sorts of disease. *Who cares? I'm going to die from a scorpion sting. Don't think about it. Breathe.*

Anna was brandishing her repellent, spray-ing through the air. And then she seemed to remember me and knelt down, spraying my neck and ears, wherever I couldn't cover up. She buttoned my shirt to the top and rolled my socks up.

I just watched, unable to use my hands. In fact, my hand was really swollen now. My fingers felt tight, and it hurt to bend them.

"Don't die!" Anna repeated. She sat beside me under the roof of palms that she'd propped against the branch above us. "What can we do?"

I pointed to the garbage bag in my pocket, and she unfolded it and wrapped it around me like a poncho.

The rain started pouring hard like a switch had been flipped. We huddled under the palm leaves, but they made a terrible roof. Water streamed in, onto my head, down my neck. Rain dripped off my nose. I felt my hair plastered to my head. The terrible pain coursed all through my hand and up my arm.

Anna cupped her hands under the stream and tried to get me to drink some, but I couldn't

even lift my head. I just lay there moaning. I couldn't be bothered to talk or move. I concentrated on taking one breath after another.

I should be in my bed at the resort with its solid roof and walls and the mosquito netting. I need my parents. They'd be able to take me to a doctor. Actually, I should be at a hospital!

Of all the times I'd had panic attacks over a strong wind, or the thought of missing the bus, or writing a test, or Noah Martin giving me a wedgie in gym class, or any number of troubling things in a day, I didn't think I'd ever been as close to dying as I was right then. Of all my worries about terrible events, I'd never imagined this would be how I'd die. In a rainforest, in the rain, in the dark.

Anna sat with her knees up to her chest, arms wrapped around her legs while the deluge went on. How long could the rain last?

"We shouldn't be here," Anna was muttering to herself. "I wish my dad was here. He'll find us."

Would anyone find us out here, in the rain? Were my parents worried now? I had to stop thinking about it. I had to stay calm.

The jungle steamed.

As suddenly as it had started, the rain stopped. But the pounding rain had at least muffled the other noises. Now we could hear night creatures all around us. There were shrieks and *pop-pop-pop*s, chirrups, grunts, bellowing. My heart stuttered as a scream erupted not far away, then trailed off. Something had died like I was going to die.

Calm. It would be morning eventually. I kept my breathing even. I recited the different birds I had on my life list. Was my hand hurting a bit less? I didn't feel so achy. My mind began to slow down. I listened to the leftover rain travel down the canopy.

Drip. Drip. Drip.

My head nodded. And then I felt delicate hands on my face.

"EEEE!" I rolled and glimpsed the tail of a skinny raccoon scurrying away.

"What?" Anna yelled. She looked around wildly, blinking. "You okay?"

"I'm okay," I said, surprised.

But for how long? We were sitting ducks out there, no fire, no shelter. I wasn't going to be able to sleep all night. And I was definitely *not* going to wonder if there were any more scorpions.

CHAPTER SIX

When I woke, the first thing I noticed was my hand didn't hurt anymore. I inspected it in the predawn light, flexing and turning it over. The fingers were back to normal. I hadn't died! I'd survived a scorpion sting!

I was able to see the jungle around us. It looked much friendlier than the dark shadows and lurking dangers of the night before.

"Anna," I said. "Anna?"

She stirred and then bolted up. She looked around. "Wasn't a dream, then?"

"No." I pulled the garbage bag off and got

up. Our palm leaves had slid off the log in the night. Worst shelter ever.

I wandered around Anna, inspecting the ground for tracks. Maybe we could follow our tracks. Who was I kidding? I didn't know how to track anything.

"We have to get back," Anna said. "My parents are going to kill me. We need to find that trail!" She swung the machete. She looked so fierce holding the knife. I wished I was more like her.

Anna started a charge forward, but then almost toppled sideways. She grabbed her head in her hand.

"You need water," I said. "All of our sweating is making us dehydrated."

We both heard the sudden rustling of branches and looked up. The white-faced monkeys were back. I eyed them while I retrieved the garbage bag and stuffed it into my largest pocket.

"What are they doing?" Anna asked.

The monkeys were taking turns at something on the ground. I cautiously stepped closer and watched them bend over a hole in the roots of the tree. It looked like a well.

"Hey, they found water."

When we hurried toward them, they scurried away.

"It's rainwater, so it's safe to drink!" I said.

We leaned over the tree well and pulled up handfuls of fresh water, slurping loudly.

"Oh, that feels better," Anna said, then wiped her mouth. "You're right, I was thirsty. Now we've got to find the trail. Come on!"

I dipped the garbage bag into the well and let the bottom fill with a few cups of water. Pulling the bulging bag out, I carefully twisted the top closed, and then tied the bag to my belt. It swung awkwardly and made sloshing noises as I moved.

"Anna, give me the machete."

When she handed it to me, I sliced it along the bark of the tree to blaze a mark. Or I tried to. The blade stuck into the bark, and I had to wriggle the machete to get it loose. I whacked harder, but it barely cut through.

"How does anyone use this thing?" I asked, swinging again. The blade slipped and grazed the thumb on my left hand.

I froze, my heart thumping at the close call. "Ah!"

My hand shook as I inspected my thumb. "Cuts in the rainforest get infected quickly because it's so moist. Breeding ground for diseases."

"You're a breeding ground for worry," Anna said, taking the machete. "Relax, it's just a scratch."

She sliced the trunk, making a small flat cut mark. The pale color stood out from the rest of the dark trunk. "Is that what you were trying to do? It's all in the wrist."

"It's so we know where we've been," I said.

Anna nodded appreciatively. "That's pretty smart."

I pulled my lip balm from my pocket and coated the scrape on my thumb with a layer to protect it. "I don't want to walk in circles. The monkeys have my flagging tape, but I read that this is also how to mark a trail in the woods. We have to remember to stop and make a blaze on a tree close enough that we can still see the last one. It will help us go in a straight line."

I applied the lip balm to my lips. When Anna stared at me, I offered it to her. "Cherry," I said.

She shrugged and smeared some on her lips too, peering around in all directions. "Which way should we go?"

Should we really try to find our way back? I wondered. *Will they be able to find us here if we wait, or should we try to find the trail?* I scanned the rainforest, the canopy, the dense vines and ferns. The sun rose in the east, but I couldn't see which direction that was. It was impossible to see the sun in here. Thick green jungle crowded in. My field of view had shrunk.

I felt paralyzed with indecision; panic was

sneaking into my brain. I wished my parents were there. I'd never had to make such an important choice. I knew survival was all about making good decisions. The difference between staying or leaving could be life or death.

I shut my eyes when I felt my heartbeat pick up. *Think. What should we do?*

CHAPTER SEVEN

"We should head downhill," I said. "That's where we'll find water, and maybe a trail?"

Anna breathed out. "Okay. Let's do that."

Moving through the jungle took a frustrating amount of time. In the humidity, even walking made us tired. And the day was only starting to heat up. I wasn't hungry, even though we hadn't eaten since lunch the day before. But we'd need more water. We took turns sipping from the bag.

Every step was treacherous. The ground was like walking on banana peels on top of pudding.

We slipped and skidded in the wet leaves and mud.

"If you start to fall, don't grab a branch," I said. "Better to fall than to put your hand on something that bites."

The white-faced monkeys followed us. "Go away!"

"I think they're just curious," Anna said.

"I'd forgive them if they brought back my emergency kit," I said.

"They did show us where the water was."

The forest was constantly moving. A shimmering blue butterfly bigger than a hummingbird flitted past my face. We skirted another giant tree with the tall roots. Along the edge of the root was a procession of leaves marching. When we peered closer, we saw it was a line of ants, each carrying a large piece of green leaf over its head.

We wiped sweat off our faces as we watched the ants. Birdcalls and other noises echoed around us, different sounds from the past night, but just as busy. Everywhere I looked there was deep green, light green, shiny green, mossy green. Wait, was that a red-legged honeycreeper? Bird three hundred and nine.

Above us I was surprised to see howler monkeys, quiet now, draped in the trees. Their long tails wrapped around branches, arms and legs dangling idly. A tiny one clutched at an adult, watching me intently.

Anna sliced a mark in the tree, and we kept going. "Why do you get panic attacks?" she asked.

"If I think too hard about things, I start to worry."

"Huh. Can't you just stop worrying?"

"I worry about worrying. I can't help it. That's what a panic attack is. The doctors took a long time to figure out it's just from anxiety."

"That sucks." Anna paused to slap at a mosquito as she hacked through a wall of vines. "I've lost my can of repellent! It must be back where we slept."

When we stepped through the vines, we saw what was ahead of us and stopped short. A herd of animals with long faces and pig snouts were rooting around in a clearing.

They raised their heads to stare with dark beady eyes. For a moment, everything froze. I crinkled my nose at the stink in the air. That was when the chaos erupted.

The animals scattered in all directions as if a cannon had gone off. They grunted and barked and clicked their teeth. It was a vicious sound like two wooden rulers slapping together. The largest one had erect, bristled hairs along its back. It eyed us with hostility and gnashed its teeth.

And then it charged right at me.

CHAPTER EIGHT

The pig thing thundered toward me. My legs turned to wood. All I could do was stand there, holding my breath, staring. My hands limp at my sides.

Bristly fur. Clacking teeth.

It got closer and closer and closer—

"Carter!" Anna screamed.

I threw my arms in front of my face. The beast veered at the last second and charged past me into the vines.

"Up here!" Anna yelled from partway up a twisted tree.

I spied a skinny tree or hard vine with knobby bulges up its length. They were like steps of a staircase. I raced upward. "Are they coming back?" I screamed.

"I don't see them anymore, but I hope not. They smell horrible." Anna pointed her machete at me from her tree. "That was a brave move, playing chicken with it."

Brave? I clutched my stair tree and gulped air. My legs quivered. It wasn't until that moment I noticed I had climbed a tree! I hadn't even stopped to worry about the danger of falling. I remembered when my friend Max talked me into climbing the tree in our backyard when we were young. He had to fetch my mom to come get me down. I vowed I'd never climb another tree.

I assessed my heart rate. Now that the danger was gone, I was actually okay. I secretly grinned. There had been no time for another panic attack.

We waited in our trees, listening to make

sure the pig things had gone. Scanning the forest, I noted I still couldn't see where we were. I would have to climb above the canopy to see farther, but that was out of the question.

A flurry of peeps and tittering noises grew louder. Something was zipping toward us through the trees.

"Squirrel monkeys!" Anna pointed.

About forty tiny bodies raced from branch to branch. They were so fast I could barely keep track of them. I watched one walking on all fours under a branch before it spied me and warily hid in the leaves.

A double-toothed kite landed on the stairs beside me, and I almost fell off from excitement. "Three hundred and ten," I whispered.

A tawny-winged woodcreeper stopped in the next tree. I took out my binoculars to make sure that's what it was. I remembered those birds followed squirrel monkeys, because they were after the insects the monkeys kicked up. I grinned. "Three eleven."

It was much easier to climb down this trunk than our backyard tree, since this one had stairs built in. I carefully maneuvered my way until my feet were on the ground. I looked up at where I had been and felt a sense of pride.

But once we continued on, I forgot about the climbing success. Sweat ran down our faces; it dripped into my eyes. It was getting too hot to move. Our water was gone. I tried to avoid thinking about what would happen if we didn't find more soon.

"Where are those white-faced monkeys now?" Anna said. "They need to show us more water. And food. We missed breakfast, and I *never* miss breakfast! What can we eat here?"

"There're probably all kinds of things, but I don't know if it's safe to eat what the monkeys are eating."

We slid down a steep hill, trying to stay upright in the slippery leaves. When we paused at the bottom, I heard something.

"Sounds like water ahead!" We sprinted toward a bubbly stream, coursing over a bed of rocks.

"At last," Anna said. She immediately knelt and cupped her hands into the water.

"Wait! We need to boil that first," I said. "I don't have my purification tablets. You could get really sick."

Anna groaned. "It looks clean to me."

"The parasites are tiny." I held up my thumb and finger pressed together to show her how small.

"Really? Something the size of a spider turd is going to make me sick?" She splashed the back of her neck. "Well, how are we going to boil it?"

I shielded my eyes from the sun. We could see it now through the break in the canopy. "I have an idea." I pulled the mini binoculars out from my shirt and studied them. "We can use one of the lenses like a magnifying glass and start a fire with the sun."

While Anna gathered twigs and leaves, I un-screwed the lens.

"What are we going to use to boil the water in? The bag will burn."

"Uh. I don't know. Are there coconuts around? We could use a coconut shell."

"No coconuts."

I realized we also needed wood for the fire. "Do you think you could cut down one of those trees?" I said, pointing to a clump of them next to the water. "Let me think about what to use as a pot."

I tilted the lens so that it captured the sun, and focused a beam of light into the leaf pile. Then I sat motionless and waited. Sweat trick-led down my nose. Tiny legs marched across the back of my neck. *Are those ants? Pretend they're just ants.* My arm ached.

Anna hacked at one of the narrow branches of the tree. "It's hollow," she said. "Oh, it's got water in it!" She dropped to the ground, try-

ing to catch the liquid leaking out. She finished cutting the branch and inspected the inside.

"It's got sections." She rolled it upside down. "I can hear more water sloshing around inside, like a coconut!"

"It's a bamboo tree." I didn't want to move the beam of light, so I asked her to bring the section to me. "We can use this as a pot to hold over the flame! See? It's like a bowl. Can you get the water out of the other section?"

Anna cut, but most of the water trickled out from her hacking. "It leaks when I hit it." She tried getting her mouth underneath to catch it in time, but the water had drained. "We have to drink the creek water. I'm so thirsty."

"Wait, I've almost made the fire." I waved my hand in front of the beam of light. The beam felt hot, but nothing was happening. I adjusted the beam to make it smaller and was encouraged with a tiny bit of smoke. "It's working!"

We stared at the pile. I expected it to burst

into flame any minute the way I'd seen it happen on YouTube. But the smoke fizzled away.

"I think the leaves are too wet," I said. "Can you find drier ones?"

"Where? Everything is wet. I'm just going to drink." Anna dunked her face in and sucked up the water.

"Don't!"

"Ahhhh!" She smacked her lips.

The slurping noises made me even thirstier. I didn't know if the fire would ever work. I really wished I had my lighter from the kit. But it was harder than I thought to start a fire in a rainforest.

"This was supposed to work," I said, trying to stay calm.

"You can't plan for everything, Carter. No one knows everything."

Her words made me uneasy. "That's what I do," I said. "I plan. I wrote a booklet at home for emergency protocols, and I make my parents hold fire drills. I have a ladder that I can hang out my bedroom window to escape. I keep a list of hurricane safety procedures in the house, how to turn off electricity and gas, that sort of thing. I boxed up a disaster supplies kit in the pantry —canned food, bottled water, battery-operated radio, flashlight, and protective clothing. I make a specific emergency kit for each place we travel. I have to know everything to feel safe."

Anna stared at me. "Well, you didn't plan on getting stung by a scorpion, and that turned out okay," she said simply. "No matter how much you plan, you have to be prepared for the unexpected. My dad always says, 'Everything you've ever wanted is on the other side of fear.'" She took another drink. "Didn't you say we should drink so we don't get dehydrated from sweating? You better have some."

The other side of fear? I'd have to think about that later. My head pounded. Maybe the danger of dehydration was worse than the danger of getting sick from drinking a parasite.

"At least it looks clean," I said, dipping my hand.

I brought it to my mouth, but then gave up and copied what Anna was doing, sticking my face in and sucking. It was cool and delicious.

After we drank, I felt better, though I wished I hadn't said all that to Anna. But my mind was clearer. I wanted to study the bamboo trees, but a commotion in the canopy distracted me.

"Monkeys are back." Anna pointed above. "And they're out of control."

They were screeching and jumping up and down. They flung fruit and branches into a tree hanging over the clump of bamboo. Something there made my guts tighten.

A giant tan colored snake with dark stripes and an arrow-shaped head.

"Boa constrictor!" I yelled.

It lay patiently in a coil on the crook of a branch. Seed balls rained down on it. The snake did not look the least bit concerned.

"I was just there cutting a tree down!" Anna

yelled. "That thing could've dropped on my head! It looks like it could swallow me whole."

For the first time, she looked like she was going to cry. But she didn't—she just got mad. "Bad snake! Get out of here!" She picked up a stone and hurled it at the boa constrictor.

Between the monkeys and the angry girl, the snake decided that wasn't the best place for a nap. It slowly uncoiled and moved to the next branch. But when it moved, we could see the bulge of something inside it.

CHAPTER NINE

"Baby monkey?" I suggested. "Maybe that's why the monkeys are so upset. We don't have to worry—these snakes are harmless to us. But we should move."

I pointed in the direction the stream was flowing. "You think this might lead to the ocean? That's our best chance of finding people."

We followed the stream. It grew wider, dropping over large rocks into several mini waterfalls. We clambered over the rocks, Anna's machete clanking as she used her hands to steady herself.

The air smelled like flowers and rain. Bees buzzed next to me, and I was amazed to notice that I didn't freak out, just waited for them to fly by. Out there, my smaller worries didn't seem as scary anymore.

Anna paused and held up a hand for me to listen. We both stared up at the canopy. Then her shoulders slumped. "Thought I heard something."

Her voice sounded small. The fierce Anna was shrinking the longer we were lost. "A rescue plane wouldn't be able to see us, would it?"

"I don't know."

"Do you think we're going to make it out of here . . . alive?"

I reached for her shoulder and gave it a squeeze. We shared a look. In that moment, something passed between us that seemed to acknowledge we were in this together. It felt like we were giving each other strength.

Anna stood straighter. I felt braver. Determination replaced the terror on her face. She nodded, dunked her head under a waterfall, and continued to lead, water streaming down her back.

Once the terrain leveled off, the banks along the stream got muddy. Anna stopped, staring at something at her feet. I peered around her at a very large print deeply imbedded in the mud.

Anna spread her hand and placed it over the print. "What has three toes and makes a track the size of two of my hands?"

"Um. Let's keep moving."

I scanned for crocodiles, but I was pretty sure they had big drag marks where their tails slid. Not square footprints. *What could make a print like that?*

The stream we were following met up with a river, but we slowed to a crawl trying to move along its bank. The trees there were short with roots that grew aboveground. Red crabs ran over the roots and scuttled away as we approached.

We had to climb over and under the roots. It was more tiring than going through the thick vegetation.

"This is starting to get hard," Anna said.

"Starting?" This was not working. What were we going to do? We were filthy and covered in mosquito bites. Our clothes were torn. I wanted to be safe at home. I wanted my parents to shake their heads at my latest emergency plan and tell me everything would be okay. I squeezed my eyes shut.

With this new obstacle, I felt myself trembling with the panic coming on. But then I considered what Anna had said about how I had to be prepared for the unexpected. And something about the other side of fear—I'd even been stung by a scorpion, and I was still there. If I could survive that, I could get past my fears.

"I wish we could just swim downriver," Anna said.

Neither of us mentioned the gigantic tracks

we'd seen in the mud. What animals could be lurking in the water?

While we stared at the river, an idea formed from something that had been bugging me since we saw the bamboo.

"Let's find more of those hollow trees," I said. "I think I know what we can do."

"First, I need to drink," Anna said.

But the river was muddy here, and even she hesitated.

"Let's make a filter," I said. "We don't have any charcoal, do we?"

"I left my stash of charcoal at home. Sorry," Anna said, giving me a flat look.

"Let's try it anyway. I practiced at home for emergencies once by making a water filter from a bag." I laid out the garbage bag on the ground and began lining the bottom with the fine silt from the riverbank.

"Look for gravel, or larger stones," I said to Anna. "We need to layer sand, and then rocks,

and then sand and rocks again like a birthday cake. Then when we pour water in the top, it filters through and comes out clean."

Once the layers were packed in, I pointed at the bag. "Anna, will you make knots on each side so we can hang it?"

Using my teeth, I unraveled the eight feet of paracord I'd used to make my survival bracelet. Then I tied it in two loops around the knots Anna had made and hung the bag from a low branch. We scooped water from the river, and then dumped it into the top of the bag. Anna poked a small hole in the bottom with her machete. After a minute, we held our hands under the water that dribbled out.

"Is it cleaner?" asked Anna, peering into her hands. "I can't tell."

"It worked better at home," I admitted. "Must need the charcoal."

After we drank, we hiked back into the jungle and found more bamboo. Along with something else I finally recognized.

"That's a termite nest!" I pointed excitedly. "We can eat them." I grinned at her expression. She grimaced back.

"And a termite nest is supposed to be good insect repellent," I said as I showed Anna how to hold a stick into the nest and wait for the termites to climb it. I bit them off my stick like I'd learned in Australia. They didn't taste like anything.

Anna scrunched her face, watching me chew. "Never thought I'd be eating bugs." Then she shrugged and copied me, biting them off her stick. "Well . . . they aren't terrible. What did you say about using them for the mosquitos?"

"Supposedly you can burn the nest and the smoke keeps them away, but we don't have any fire." I picked at the hard, holey nest, and smelled the dust under my nail. It was woody, almost spicy. "We could try just rubbing it on our skin?" I suggested.

Anna hacked a chunk off the nest and created tiny termite chaos. We each crumbled a piece

in our hands, some termites still clinging to it. I rubbed the crumbs and the termites all over the back of my neck and face. It did seem to keep the mosquitos off.

"This was a good idea, Carter. I wish I was as smart as you."

She wished she was like me? I watched Anna rub dust over her face. She clapped her hands to get rid of the dust, and then punched me in the arm.

"Stop staring at me, nerd." She smiled.

I wished I was fearless like her.

CHAPTER TEN

As Anna ate more termites, I explained my plan. She listened while she chewed. "But you're sure it will float?"

"If we use the hollow bamboo trees, they'll float. We'll need to cut some of these skinny hanging vines to use as rope." I'd used all my paracord on the water filter.

"If we use five or six trees, and then brace them with cross pieces, it might be wide enough to be stable and long enough for the two of us, like a canoe."

Anna reached up and yanked a vine down. "How do you know all this stuff? You couldn't have read all this before you came here."

"My grandpa makes canoes and boats. I like to watch and help. Well, I don't help. I'm . . ." I rubbed my face in embarrassment. "I'm afraid of the power tools."

Anna knelt with the vine and started pulling it apart.

"I just like being in Grandpa's shop," I continued. "It always smells like sawdust and glue and the goopy stuff he puts in his hair. It makes me feel calm, I guess, to be with him. And I love painting the boats." I glanced at Anna to see if she understood.

She sat back on her heels and picked her teeth. "It might work."

"Do you think you can get us six of those?" I pointed to a batch of bamboo trees with long, straight stems. They were narrow enough to cut down, about the width of a flagpole.

Anna jumped up, looking excited by the

plan. By the time I had the vine strands weaved together to make cord, she had the first tree down.

"How are you so strong?" I asked, wishing I could cut down a tree. Watching her made me feel even more hopeless.

She shrugged. "I like sports. I've been playing basketball since I was seven. And I was the only girl on the wrestling team. I had to learn to defend myself. Also I licked the monkey statue, remember?" She winked at me. "I know it was made up, but I thought it would be fun." Her face clouded. She bent to hack at the next tree as if she wasn't afraid of anything.

I thought of all the things I'd been afraid of happening since I was old enough to worry. Of all the times I'd imagined something like the situation we were in now. I'd been so scared of all the things that could go wrong. Well, everything *did* go wrong, and I was still alive, even after getting stung by a scorpion. Maybe *I'd* gotten strong from licking the monkey too.

After we dragged the trees down to the river-bank, I lined up the bamboo pieces and studied them. They had to fit tightly together. When I tried flipping one around, I tripped and ended up rolling over and then under most of the logs. I landed in the mud, half in the water. Anna hid her grin.

I picked up the vine to tie the cross pieces. Each log should be individually tied. As I thought about how it would work, I imagined all the ways I could screw it up. What if I didn't tie them right and our raft broke apart? We'd be dumped into the river with crocodiles and large animals with three toes.

My fingers felt awkward, and my knots got all tangled. The rope didn't work right. Nothing stayed together properly. It looked so easy watching Grandpa.

"Can I try?" Anna held her hand out for the vine.

"Loop that end over." I pointed to the vine.

"Good. Then hitch this close and pry it so it's tight. No . . . the other way—yeah!"

I instructed as Anna tied. Once the cross-beams were secured for support, our raft almost looked like a seaworthy vessel that Grandpa might make. "Now we need a couple poles to push with," I said. "Long ones."

I glanced up at the sun. It was late afternoon already. I couldn't believe how fast the day had gone. Remembering how quickly it got dark the night before, I knew we needed to hurry.

We launched the raft by rolling it through the mud until it floated. I danced on shore for a few steps, trying to find the courage to get on. Anna jumped onboard and did a cautious test bounce. The raft wobbled, but stayed afloat.

"We're awesome!" she yelled, and held her hand out to high-five.

I carefully stepped on, holding my pole. My legs felt shaky and my heart thumped, but I did it. We sat cross-legged near the center and stabilized. Grandpa would be proud.

I was relieved how much easier it was to travel on the river. The shoreline drifted past. We poled to keep the raft from spinning, but mostly the current kept us moving. Soon the shoreline passed a little faster. The raft bobbed harder. We came to a bend in the river, and then really picked up speed. My breath came out in a gasp.

We ran through a stretch of jumbled, swirly water. The side of my pants got soaked from a splash. The raft bounced crazily, and Anna almost toppled off. I grabbed her, and we held on. The machete slid off and sank out of view before either of us could save it. My hand clutched hers.

I glanced nervously around at the jungle speeding by. That was when I saw the rapids in front of us. Anna and I locked eyes.

"Hang on," I screamed.

CHAPTER ELEVEN

We crashed through the rapids, barely missing a large rock sticking out. The raft tipped like a bucking horse, but we dodged to the other side. Water sprayed over us as the raft smashed back down. We balanced in the center of the raft, drenched to our eyeballs, clutching the sides of the bamboo.

With the logs jostling, the movement worked the knots in the vines loose. One of the logs broke away. I reached for it, but it slipped out of the lashing and was gone before I could grab it.

"Oh, no!" Anna yelled.

With only five logs, our raft was even more narrow and tippy. We were barely out of the water; our feet kept sliding off and trailing in the river. I desperately tried to forget that crocodiles can grow up to twenty feet long and kill one tourist every year. *Please let there not be any crocodiles.*

I yanked the lashings tighter that were holding the rest of the raft together. The remaining logs stayed snug. But what if there were more rapids ahead? We'd tip for sure.

I pulled the garbage bag out of my pocket. "Help me make a drogue."

"A what?"

"We sailed in Newfoundland on a puffin watching trip. The water got rough, and the captain used a big parachute thing behind the boat to steady it. He called it a drogue."

The garbage bag was already tied with my paracord. But the cord was too short to let the bag drag far enough behind if it was tied to the raft. I handed Anna one line. "We'll have to hold our lines like flying a kite, okay?"

I saw more rough water ahead. "Hurry!"

Together we let out the garbage bag to the ends of our lines, and then hung on. The garbage bag dragged behind like a dark open mouth, full of water.

We went through the rough water more slowly this time. We still got soaked from the spray, but the raft didn't bounce as much, and our progress was steadier down the river.

"It's working!" Anna said.

I wiped the water off my face and looked around. The jungle surrounding us was alive. Birds flitted in the trees, filling the air with their calls. Shadows moved. A metallic beetle flew past me.

I pointed at a giant lizard baking in the sun. As we drifted toward an overhanging branch, a large dark monkey lowered itself and hung by only its tail. It stared solemnly at us, its long arms hanging by its sides.

"Spider monkey," Anna whispered. She pointed to her sweat-soaked, green T-shirt that read CORCOVADO NATIONAL PARK and had monkeys with long arms peeking out from behind the letters. She really was all about the monkeys.

Slowly, the monkey extended an arm over its head, and pulled itself into the branches without a sound. A small lizard zipped by, tiptoeing across the top of the water. There was so much going on in the jungle.

But the best part of being on the river was the breeze. It aired out my quick-dry shirt that had been stuck to me all day. It felt like a fan in a stuffy room, blowing the hot air around, but it was better than being in the middle of the jungle.

"Carter!" Anna pointed at something in the water, and my heart skipped.

A very large, dark animal was swimming toward us in a straight line at an alarming pace. Was that a gigantic crocodile? It could snap our tiny raft in half with one bite.

Anna clutched my arm, her face white with fear. "Is it going to eat us?" she whispered.

When I scanned the water, I couldn't see it. I spun around, searching. After all we'd been through making it out of the jungle, were we going to be attacked by a crocodile?

I twisted to my right, and there it was. It rose from the river, water streaming off its enormous body. It must've weighed seven or eight hundred pounds.

"Oh!" Anna said.

It was not a crocodile.

CHAPTER TWELVE

The animal stood, staring at us. It looked like a cross between a giant pig and an elephant. The weird dangling nose sniffed the air. Then the animal turned and crept into the forest, disappearing into the tangle of branches.

We were silent a moment. Anna let out a breath. "You think that has three toes?" she asked.

"Yeah, that's what made those tracks," I said. "I should've known. It's a Baird's tapir. My mom hoped to see one while we were here. She called them gentle giants."

A hot feeling of homesickness stabbed me in the guts. My parents were searching for me, worrying, probably really mad and scared. I wanted so badly to see them again. I wanted to tell them all the things I'd done out there. And I wanted to be home.

Our river soon emptied out to the ocean. There was a beach on our right. As we drifted closer, I eyed the larger waves on the shore.

The raft hit the wave, and rode right over top. We came to a landing with a hiss, and jumped off on wobbly legs. I flopped into the soft sand, Anna collapsing next to me. We'd made it out of the jungle!

"Can you believe the monkeys gave you back the one thing you needed most from your kit? The garbage bag," Anna said. "It's like they knew all the things we'd use it for."

I glanced at the bag, fluttering lightly beneath the raft. It had made a good drogue, a water bottle, a filter, and a rain poncho. We could have used it as a ground tarp and even a sail for our raft.

"Look what I found." Anna held up a smooth green coconut from where she lay.

We looked around and noticed there were coconuts everywhere. Using a sharp rock, Anna cracked open a hole in the top of one, and we took turns drinking from it. I sat back in the sand and suddenly felt exhausted. We stayed like that for a moment, looking out at the colors on the ocean. The sun was starting to set, creating a soft glow on the ocean, and the breeze felt so nice on my hot skin.

"There's your spirit protector." Anna pointed to the branches above me.

I spun and saw the resplendent quetzal. The bird twitched and then flew away. I gave a little gasp to see it showing off shimmering, dazzling colors in the setting sun.

"Spirit protector of Mayan warriors," I said. "You're more of a warrior than me."

"You're the one who knows all the stuff for us to get through the jungle. We never would have made it here without all your reading. You're a warrior. You're like a knowledge warrior."

I thought about that. About all the things I'd done that I never knew I could. About how some of my plans worked, and some didn't but I had come up with new plans. Then I remembered the animals with clacking teeth. "I have to tell you . . . I wasn't actually brave back there."

"Back where?"

"With the pig things. I was just too afraid to move. I'm not brave like you. You're fearless."

Anna chuckled. "I am *not* fearless. I was just as scared in the jungle as you, but we had to keep going. You were scared, but you kept going. We made it to the other side of fear. That's what being brave is. Quetzal Power?" She held her fist out toward me, and I bumped it with mine.

"Quetzal Power," I repeated.

We grinned at each other and then fell silent.

And then we both heard it.

Voices. Human voices.

We leaped up and bolted down the beach. Breathless, we reached the spit of sand and were able to see into the bay. Three boats were pulled up on shore, and there were fishermen cleaning nets. They were packing up to leave. We raced toward them, waving our arms and screeching like howler monkeys.

CHAPTER THIRTEEN

Six weeks later.

"Then the fishermen took you back to the resort?" asked the reporter.

"Yeah." I shuddered at the memory of the resort. "It was like a circus with all the searchers. They'd been trying to find us all day and the night before. It's hard to find someone in the jungle unless you know exactly where to look."

I thought back to the moment I had reached my mom and dad. How we all hugged and cried together in a huddle. How relieved they were.

They hadn't been mad; they'd been proud. My throat tightened, and I focused back on the reporter.

"That was a smart move, marking your trail. If anyone had found where you guys camped, they could've followed it." The reporter nodded at me. "And I bet Anna is impressed with you. I like that she called you a knowledge warrior. Fitting."

My face suddenly felt hot. "We did it together. But surviving being lost has helped me. It taught me something. The jungle has dangers as small as pinheads, yet harmless animals as big as cars. There's danger and awesome things mixed together. Just like living here with all the hurricanes."

"And how are your panic attacks now, since your ordeal?" the reporter asked.

"I don't get them anymore. Well, I do still feel myself getting worried about stuff if I let my imagination go. But then I remember that I can plan for the unexpected. I remember what the jungle taught me, that not everything is trying to kill me. I don't worry about little things as much as I used to. I'm learning to manage my anxiety better."

The other toddler Mom was babysitting shrieked in excitement. I raised my hands, showing I hadn't flinched. "See?"

"Impressive—"

"Hey, guys!" Dad called down the stairs to us. "The slide show is ready. Are you almost done?"

"Hope you have two hours to look at bird pictures," I said. "The ones with the resplendent quetzal are amazing."

The reporter looked alarmed. "Actually, I have to run. But I have one more question. Did you find out about that scorpion bite? How did you survive it?"

"It wasn't a bad kind of scorpion. The pain usually only lasts an hour, unless you're allergic. Lucky me. I didn't get so lucky with the parasites though."

"What parasites?"

"The water Anna and I drank. Gave us both the runs pretty bad until we started the medication. Anna thought it was hilarious." I shook my head and smiled. "And that girl says *I'm* weird!"

AUTHOR'S NOTE

This story was inspired by dozens of accounts of hikers lost in the rainforests of Costa Rica. No one believes it will happen to them until it does. Anyone wandering in the jungle does not have to go far off the trail to get turned around in the thick vegetation.

One couple went for a short hike in the Osa Peninsula region and veered off the trail to see a special tree. They were not lost, but the woman tripped and broke an ankle. The man went to get help. When he returned, he could not find where he had left his wife. They searched for three weeks before they found her. Unfortunately, it was too late.

As with all of the books in this series, I am most fascinated by the stories of survival. I read about two hikers who managed to stay alive for seven weeks after they tried to blaze their own trail through the jungle. What made the difference for them? They mostly ate spiders, but both lost significant weight. One man became extremely ill. Yet they continued on and made it out.

I was also amazed to discover someone I work with had been lost with his friend for weeks in the Cloud Forest Reserve near Monteverde. They had tried to follow a new trail that was badly marked. Eventually, they wandered off of it and were left with only a photocopy of an old map and their wits. They ran out of food. They became dehydrated.

During my interview with him, I heard one of the important details that allowed them to survive—they did not panic. They did not talk about their fears. They just kept at the job of finding their way out, approached it like a logic problem. They stayed calm.

I wondered how easy it would be to stay calm with the possibility of never making it out of the jungle alive. This led me to consider — what if someone who had anxiety about everyday life got lost and had to find his way out? How would he survive?

While this story was inspired by true events, and every effort was made to keep to the facts, some details are fictional, including the names of the characters and some settings.

SO WHAT CAN YOU DO TO BE PREPARED?

BUILD YOUR OWN SURVIVAL KIT: COURTESY OF THE CANADIAN RED CROSS

Emergency situations can be scary, but if you are prepared for the unexpected, you can move beyond fear and deal with any kind of situation with confidence.

From the Canadian Red Cross, here are ten essentials to put in your backcountry survival kit:

1. Knife: preferably with locking blade

2. Fire-making supplies: lighter, matches, fire starter (can be homemade—e.g., cotton balls coated in petroleum jelly), candle

95

3. Whistle: shrill enough to penetrate up-wind through a storm, and will work cold or wet

4. Navigation aids: compass and map, watch

5. Sun protection: sunblock, lip balm, sunglasses, and hat

6. First-aid kit: Band-Aids, tweezers, antiseptic wipes, antibiotic ointment, pain relief tablets, safety pins, sling, hydrocortisone cream

7. Food and water bottle: energy bar or trail mix and filtered water

8. Clothing: dry socks, wool beanie

9. Light: mini flashlight with battery

10. Shelter-making material: garbage bag, tarp, or space blanket, and cordage

MORE INFORMATION CAN BE FOUND AT THESE WEBSITES:

American Red Cross Emergency preparedness: www.redcross.org/get-help/prepare-for-emergencies/be-red-cross-ready/get-a-kit

Canadian Red Cross Emergency preparedness: www.redcross.ca/how-we-help/emergencies-and-disasters-in-canada/for-home-and-family/get-a-kit

U.S. Department of Homeland Security preparedness: www.ready.gov/kit

Northwest Territories Parks wilderness survival tips: nwtparks.ca/be-prepared/wilderness-survival-tips

ACKNOWLEDGMENTS

In my research for this book, I collected information from many sources, including books, videos, articles, and journals. I am grateful for Randy Tippin and Blake Piche for allowing me to interview them and for sharing their stories with me. Blake, your bravery was an inspiration.

Thank you to my critique partners, Marcia Wells, Amy Fellner Dominy, and Sylvia Musgrove, who provided feedback and encouragement.

Any errors in the story are my own.

ABOUT THE AUTHOR

Terry Lynn Johnson has lived in northern Ontario, Canada, for more than forty years. She was the owner and operator of a dogsledding business with eighteen huskies. She guided overnight trips and taught winter survival. During the school year, she taught dogsledding at an outdoor school near Thunder Bay, Ontario.

She currently works as a conservation officer with the Ontario Ministry of Natural Resources and Forestry. Before becoming a conservation officer, she worked for twelve years as a canoe ranger warden in Quetico Provincial Park, a large wilderness park in northwestern Ontario.

In her free time, Terry enjoys traveling to new places. Among her adventures, she's hiked a volcano in Saint Kitts and explored the jungle, Coba ruins, and *cenotes* (natural swimming holes) of Mexico's Yucatan. In Costa Rica she kayaked through mangroves, went whitewater rafting near Arenal, and waterfall rappelling and canyoneering in Quepos. She hiked Manuel Antonio National Park, where she was nearly mugged by white-faced monkeys working together in a group like organized crime. And during an evening hike, she was chased out of the jungle by the eerie calls of howler monkeys. She can't wait to go back.

Here's a sneak peek at the next book in the
SURVIVOR DIARIES series: *DUST STORM!*

SURVIVOR DIARIES

DUST STORM!

Stay calm.
Stay smart.
Survive.

TERRY LYNN JOHNSON

CHAPTER ONE

"Were you afraid?" The reporter set his phone on the coffee table in front of me and pressed the Record button.

"Of course she was," Ma Ma said, rocking faster in her chair.

I rubbed at a spot on my jeans. My grandparents did not like this story, and I didn't want Ma Ma hearing the details again.

"Aya," she muttered.

My grandfather placed his hand on her knee and her frantic rocking slowed. "Let Jen tell it," he said calmly.

"She's a strong, smart girl," Ma Ma said to the reporter. "That's all you need to know."

"Yes, Mrs. Chiu," agreed the reporter. "But I'd like to hear the account in Jen's words. I'm writing a series about resourceful kids like her who have survived a life-threatening experience."

He turned his gaze to me just as I was reaching for one of the mini cream puffs sitting in Mom's fancy dish, the one that she only uses when guests are here. We don't usually have sweets like this. I popped a pastry in my mouth.

The reporter leaned across the coffee table toward me. "Go on and tell me about what happened in the Chihuahua Desert," he said.

"It was so craz—" a piece of cream puff flew out of my mouth and landed on his phone.

"Aya," Ma Ma said.

I clamped a hand over my mouth as I swallowed. "I mean . . . it was intense. The air was so full of sand—it felt like a million bees stinging. The wind screamed around us. Grit got into my eyes, up my nose. We couldn't see anything. I'll never forget the roar just before . . ."

"Jen," the reporter interrupted. "I'd really like to hear the whole story. Start from the beginning. It will help readers know what to do if something like this happens to them. So tell me"—his eyebrows rose—"how did you survive?"

I thought about that day. Brought my mind back to the endless desert in New Mexico. Back to the heat and the fear and the terrible thirst.

"It all started with the Snake Byte," I began.